TWIG C. GEORGE

Swimming

with

SHARKS

ILLUSTRATED BY YONG CHEN

HARPERCOLLINS*PUBLISHERS*

I gratefully acknowledge
Dr. Samuel H. Gruber, Professor of Marine Biology
and Fishes, Rosenstiel School of Marine
and Atmospheric Sciences, University of Miami,
and Director of the Bimini Biological Field Station;
and Dr. Alan Henningsen, Senior Aquarist,
National Aquarium in Baltimore.

SWIMMING WITH SHARKS
Text copyright © 1999 by Twig C. George
Illustrations copyright © 1999 by Yong Chen

Library of Congress Cataloging-in-Publication Data
George, Twig C.
    Swimming with sharks / Twig C. George ; illustrated by Yong Chen.
        p.   cm.
    Summary: While spending the summer in the Florida Keys with her grand-
father, a retired marine biologist, ten-year-old Sarah has the opportunity to
observe a variety of sharks and their behavior.
    ISBN 0-06-027757-2. — ISBN 0-06-027758-0 (lib. bdg.)
    [1. Sharks—Fiction.   2. Florida Keys (Fla.)—Fiction.   3. Grandfathers—
Fiction.]   I. Chen, Yong, ill.   II. Title.
PZ7.G29343Sw   1999   98-41741
[Fic]—dc21   CIP
                                                                          AC

Typography by Elynn Cohen
3   4   5   6   7   8   9   10
❖
First Edition

For my father, John L. George;
my husband, David M. Pittenger;
and my grandfather
Frank Craighead, Sr.;
all of whom have dedicated themselves
to the preservation of wildlife
and wild places.
—T.C.G.

For Tyler Vogt —
Enjoy!

2003

Contents
▼▼▼

1
▼▼▼

Trapped for the Summer

Sarah Marshall was hot, bored and angry.

"I just wish Mom had asked me what *I* wanted to do this summer!" Sarah grumbled to a big, brown pelican who sat near her on the old dock. "I could be having fun with all my friends at camp." She paused, and the pelican turned his head as if he were waiting for her to continue. Despite herself Sarah had to laugh at the bird's knowing expression.

"Oh, great," she said in mock desperation. "Now I'm talking to a pelican. Well, at least *you* listen to me!"

Sarah stared out at the islands that seemed

to stretch endlessly across Florida Bay. Then she turned back to the pelican and mimicked her mother's voice. "It's only one summer, dear. Granddad hasn't been the same since his retirement. He's not eating well and seems so down. I know that having a nice young person like you around will help cheer him up." And so, without further discussion, Sarah's mother had arranged for her to spend the summer with her grandparents.

Scanning the popcorn-shaped clouds building along the horizon, Sarah watched a ribbon of snowy egrets skim over the trees. Normally she would have enjoyed these sights—anybody would. But Sarah felt trapped. The beautiful view, the glittering sea were just a nice setting for a terrible vacation.

She glanced around her. Her grandparents' house was very different from the new vacation homes she had passed on the drive down from Miami. It was a simple one-story house built on stilts. The house was neat but it had a "repaired" look. Even the dock was crooked and weathered.

Sarah's grandparents got by with very few

modern appliances. Dr. Joseph Santos had grown up during the Great Depression and had not forgotten what it was like to be poor. He rarely spent money on anything that was not absolutely necessary. They didn't even have a television! She could not imagine living here for six weeks, much less fifty years.

With a scowl Sarah dove off the dock into the eighty-degree water. It was warm but still cool enough to be refreshing. A little less grumpy after her swim, Sarah lay down on the dock. Her dark hair curled quickly as it dried in the sun. She watched the water drip off her fingers and make dark spots on the parched wood.

Sarah's grandfather stood at the other end of the sun-bleached dock expertly cleaning some fish. Dr. Santos was a retired marine biologist who had specialized in the study of sharks. It was a job that had been so much a part of him that he had never thought of it as work. It was who he was and what he did. Since retirement last year he had felt a little bored and uncertain. These were not feelings he was used to or liked. He missed his students and his work.

Dr. Santos loved his family and his grandchildren. Over the years, however, he and his wife, Edie, had grown used to their childless, orderly life. Sarah's arrival was proving to be much more of a challenge than he had expected. The day she arrived, she made it clear that she was not happy about staying with them for the summer. She wouldn't talk about school and gave only the simplest answers when he asked about her parents. Studying, catching, even swimming with sharks seemed like much easier tasks to him than befriending his ten-year-old granddaughter.

He finished scaling the last of the fish and threw a handful of scraps to the pelican. The pelican gobbled them up and waddled over for more. He tossed the pelican a few more pieces of fish. Then he shooed the big bird away and walked toward Sarah.

Sarah sat up, crossed her ankles and swung her legs back and forth. She wrinkled her rounded nose, which was already turning slightly red under her golden tan. One of the few things her grandfather had learned from Sarah this week was that she hated her nose. He felt it gave her a special character all her own. Spunky kid, he thought proudly. Smart, too. They would manage somehow.

He dropped the remaining fish scraps in the water. Fish appeared instantly.

"Atta girl!" he cheered, kneeling down to see something in the water. Sarah turned and gazed in the direction her grandfather was pointing.

"Watch that little damselfish go after that yellowtail!" Her grandfather watched fish like other grandfathers watched football games.

Sarah had to smile at her grandfather's enthusiasm. The fierce damselfish was one of his favorites. Sarah reluctantly moved so she could see the bright yellow warrior clearly.

"Remember these?" her grandfather asked, pointing out a swarm of small fish feeding on the scraps he had thrown them.

"French grunts, mangrove snappers and . . ." Sarah paused, trying to remember the name of the little black-and-white striped fish. "I know, sergeant majors!"

"Good," her grandfather said, as if she were a student he was testing.

Sarah knew these fish well. Ever since she was

little, her grandfather had told her their names over and over when she came to visit. She sensed it was his way of showing he cared for her, so she had learned them. Her grandfather's head ducked and weaved as he followed the scene below. Fish were his life. Her smile faded. They weren't hers, however.

No TV, no friends, nothing but fish, Sarah thought hopelessly. She took a deep breath and prepared herself for the most boring summer of her life.

2
▼▼▼

A Shark
Gives Birth

Not far from where Sarah sat on the dock, a large, female lemon shark moved across the shallow waters of Florida Bay. Seventeen years old and nine feet long, she glided over patches of white sand and turtle grass. As she swam toward the dock her senses registered many things.

Her internal ears, two pin-sized holes on either side of her head, recognized the moan of a powerboat passing in the channel. She heard the splash ten-year-old Sarah made as she jumped off the dock into the water to get some relief from the afternoon heat.

She smelled the tissue and blood from the fish Sarah's grandfather was cleaning.

She could feel objects nearby with her lateral lines. Without touching them, she felt the presence of small fish as they swam past her. She felt a sea turtle startle and move to safer waters. She felt the presence of a sunken boat hull. Without looking, she turned to avoid it.

Very little went unnoticed by the shark. On her head tiny jelly-filled pores helped her to find her way through the vast ocean. They also sensed the presence of other live animals. They signaled her that a large stingray lay buried under the sand beneath her. She didn't see it or hear it or smell it. Her pores scanned it as she passed over. Though the stingray was hidden from sight, she knew it was there. On another day she might have dug it up with her nose and eaten it. Today she swam over it. She wasn't hungry.

The lemon shark moved in rhythm with the sea that surrounded her. Slowly, steadily, she made her way toward the red mangrove trees. The mangroves grew on the islands and in the shallow waters around the edge of Florida Bay.

Thick, woody roots reached down from their branches and formed a tangled maze below the waterline. Thousands of young marine animals made this protective maze their home. It was to this ocean nursery the female shark was heading. She had come for a very special reason. She had come to give birth.

The female lemon shark stopped on the opposite side of the cove from Sarah. Her body was motionless except for the opening and closing of her mouth and the pulsing of her gills.

Her sides began to contract and her tail swung from side to side as she delivered thirteen perfect copies of herself. They slid into the world tail first. Each two-foot-long baby lemon shark was born with an umbilical cord and a yolk sac placenta. This system had nourished them through the twelve months they had grown inside their mother. Fish quickly surrounded the shark pups to feed on the cord and other tissue that they no longer needed. In a very short time there was nothing left to show that an ancient ritual had taken place along the edge of the mangroves.

The mother lemon shark, having given birth, turned and swam out to deeper water. The little lemon sharks were left to survive on their own in the shallows near the mangroves.

Without warning an osprey dove at the pups. The newly born sharks scattered. One squirmed desperately as the osprey's talons stabbed through its skin. The osprey struggled to lift the shark pup into the air. Briefly its talons lost their hold. In that instant the small shark wriggled free and instinctively darted deep into the mangroves. It had a gash in its side. The thick, waxy leaves and tangled roots of the trees did their job. The osprey lost sight of the shark and with a scream flew off without its prey.

3
▼▼▼

Sarah's Shark
Surprise

Sarah awoke early the next day. She looked
out toward the dock from her bedroom win-
dow. Her grandfather was already up. He was
standing at his fish table untangling hooks and
rinsing his fishing gear. She could see his hands
working. They were gnarled like old wood, and
the end of one pinkie shot off to the side. He
had broken it long ago and never bothered to
get it fixed.

"Too busy," he had said when Sarah asked him
why. That was about the extent of their conver-
sations unless, of course, they were about fish.

Even though his little finger was bent, his

hands moved quickly and surely, familiar with all the things they touched. As she looked harder, she saw a cloud of insects surrounding him. This was an amazing thing about her grandfather. If Sarah were to go out on the dock now, in the early morning, she would be covered with mosquitoes and tiny, biting flies called "no-see-ums." Within minutes she would be forced back into the house with welts all over her. But her grandfather just stood there and didn't seem to notice the bugs. He didn't seem to be bothered by the things that annoyed most people, like bugs, heat and the smell of fish bait. And he loved things that most people overlooked, like the battle of the little damselfish. Sarah had to admit he was interesting.

Sarah watched as her grandfather carried cameras and fishing equipment to the boat. Since retirement he spent his days on the water fishing, taking pictures and catching, measuring and releasing sharks. Officially he was retired, but watching him, you would never know it. If she asked, she could probably go with him. But why should she have to ask?

Couldn't he ask her just once? Besides, after a few hours it would get too hot out in the boat, and Granddad didn't tolerate complainers. Her grandfather didn't seem to care about *her* at all. All he cared about was fish, fish, fish!

Sarah heard her grandmother in the kitchen down the hall. She was making breakfast now. Sarah's family had spent short vacations with her grandparents since she was little. It was a slow and quiet life, with its own unique routines that never seemed to change. It was nice . . . for a week.

The boat engine chugged as it left the dock. Her brow wrinkled and she thought of school and home. Sarah thought about her friends. Her eyes filled with tears. She wiped them with the edge of her sheet and climbed out of bed. Sarah dressed slowly, walked to the kitchen and slumped into her chair.

"Good morning, sweet sunshine," sang Grandma, "good morning to you!" She said this in a singsongy voice every single morning. Sarah managed to smile and reached out to give her grandmother a hug.

It's as hard to be grumpy around Grandma as it is to be friendly around Granddad, thought Sarah.

"Your breakfast is all ready," said Grandma cheerfully as she put a large piece of fried fish on a plate in front of Sarah. Next she handed Sarah a glass of freshly squeezed orange juice. Despite herself, Sarah began to feel hungry. There was nothing as good as Grandma's fried fish, except maybe her sticky buns: big, fat, sweet buns dripping with caramelized sugar and nuts. Her mouth watered just thinking about them.

The radio was on every morning so Grandma could hear the news. Sarah listened to the comfortable voice of the newscaster and ate her breakfast quickly.

"Done already?" exclaimed her grandmother. "Why don't you take those leftovers out to the dock and feed the fish?"

This was another routine. About the time Sarah finished her breakfast, the wind usually picked up and blew the bugs away until sunset. After she finished eating, Sarah would take out the leftovers and feed the fish. Then she would

explore the inlet with her mask, snorkel and fins until she got hungry again.

Grandma watched Sarah walk out to the dock. She knew Sarah was homesick, and her heart went out to her granddaughter.

As soon as Sarah leaned over the water, the fish appeared.

"You know the routine as well as I do," she said to the fish as she broke off bits of food and dropped them into the water. She always did this carefully so that the little fish got as much as the bigger ones. Then she lay down to watch.

As Sarah observed the world below, she forgot to feel sorry for herself. Soon another fish arrived. It was bigger and yellowish brown. It had two dorsal fins on its back and a flattened head. It was about two feet long, and its head swung from side to side as it swam. It circled a piece of Grandma's fried fish, bit it and spit it out.

"I don't believe it," said Sarah aloud. "I never knew anything that didn't like Grandma's fish!"

After a minute the odd-looking fish tried it again. This time it swallowed the cooked fish.

"That's better," Sarah said firmly to the new-comer.

It swam into the shadow of the dock. Sarah had never seen a fish like this before. She ran back to the house.

"There's a new fish, Grandma," said Sarah quickly. "Can I have some more leftovers to feed it?"

"A new fish?" Grandma teased. "I thought Granddad had taught you every fish in this bay! Here, take these."

"Thanks, Grandma," Sarah called as she ran out the door.

At the ramp to the dock Sarah slowed down. She walked carefully so she wouldn't scare away her newfound fish. She lay down gingerly and dropped a morsel into the water. After a few minutes the fish reappeared. Sarah noticed it had a scar on its side. Something out there had tried to make a meal of it. A bird? A barracuda?

The fish ate its fill and then swam off toward the mangroves.

Sarah grabbed her mask and snorkel and skillfully entered the warm bay without a splash. She swam past a swirl of yellowtails and then saw the shadow of a big, silvery fish almost invisible in the underwater light. It was a tarpon. This was one of her favorite fish. She looked closer and four more appeared. They were each about three feet long with large eyes, an upturned jaw and big silvery scales. Sarah followed the school of tarpon. They circled around her. Soon she was spinning and spinning as she watched them circle and watch her in turn. When she became so dizzy she couldn't tell up from down, she stopped. As Sarah regained her balance, the tarpon continued to circle her until they were no longer interested and left. Sarah headed across the white sand of the inlet.

Dazzling lights reflected all around her. Small fish darted into the turtle grass as she passed over them. Upside-down jellyfish pulsed on the bottom. Granddad had told her that these jellyfish grew algae inside their bodies in the bright light.

"That's an easy way to get a meal," observed Sarah as she passed over their lacy forms. "Grow your own."

Then she reached the edge of the mangrove

roots. The change was immediate and magnificent. The open, sandy area she had just crossed was a desert compared with the mangroves. The shadowy mangroves teemed with fish of all kinds: young mangrove snappers, yellow tangs, grunts and what seemed like billions of other species. All small, all there to seek safety among the tangled roots. Sarah saw bright orange sea stars and coppery crabs. She swam slowly along the mangroves' edge. She was careful not to disturb the silt at the base of the roots. The slightest touch would have made clouds of mud erupt and spoil her view.

At the end of the inlet, just before it opened out into the bay, she saw a fish like the one she had just discovered at the dock. It was deep in the shadows. An even pumping of its mouth forced water across its gills, which pulsed open and closed. It was sleek, but it didn't seem to have shiny scales like other fish. Motionless, it watched her. As Sarah tried to get closer, it turned. Sarah saw the scar. It *was* her fish. At that instant she also realized what kind of fish it was. There was no doubt. The flat head, hooked fin and low-slung mouth could only be one thing: *a shark*!

Sarah stared at the shark without moving or breathing. An instant later the shark disappeared into the maze of roots with just the slightest swing of its tail. Sarah continued to stare. Finally she turned and headed home. Had she imagined the whole thing?

4
▼▼▼

Shark Bait
for Granddad

The next morning Sarah ran out to the dock
to feed the fish. As always, the "regulars"
were there waiting for her. She fed them slowly
as she waited for the little shark. She didn't
have to wait long until the oval shadow
appeared. Sarah looked carefully this time. It
was real. She couldn't believe she hadn't recognized it when she first saw it. A shark. Sarah
had her own shark!

The shark learned quickly. After just a few
days it was waiting to be fed with the other
fish. As soon as she finished feeding the fish,
Sarah would gather her snorkeling gear and

follow the shark back to the mangroves.

Then one morning Granddad stayed home to work on the boat engine. This was exactly what Sarah had been waiting for.

"Granddad," Sarah called as she headed to the dock with her plate of leftovers. "Come see my new fish. It's been coming every morning. It's not like the others."

Curious, Sarah's grandfather wiped his hands on an old rag and walked over to the dock. The reflection on the water made it hard for him to see the fish under the surface. With a grunt, he lay down next to her.

"All right, now where is this mysterious fish?" he asked.

"Here, I'll feed it. It always waits under the dock in the shade."

Sarah took a piece of fish and waved it over the water. There was a swirl and a fin broke the surface. The fish appeared for its feeding, as promised.

Sarah's grandfather squinted his eyes. "Well, I'll be . . ." he said, amazed. "It's a shark!"

"I know, Granddad," Sarah answered, with just the slightest roll of her eyes. "I've been feeding it every day. It's trained."

"Trained?" her grandfather said in a tone of voice that clearly showed he did not believe her.

"Really," Sarah insisted. "It comes every day at the same time."

"Incredible," was all Sarah's grandfather could say.

"Do you know what kind it is?" asked Sarah.

"A lemon shark. A young one, too. They're born around here at about this time of year. Your fish is probably no more than a month old, maybe less. You've done something quite special." Looking right at her, he grinned. It was the first time she'd seen her grandfather smile at anything other than a fish since she'd arrived.

"I followed it," Sarah said as she looked toward the mangroves and then up at her grandfather. This was going better than she'd planned.

"You followed a shark?" Sarah's grandfather asked suspiciously.

"I know where it lives," Sarah said, knowing she held an important piece of information. She finally had her grandfather's full attention.

"You do?" he replied, truly astonished.

"I've found it a bunch of times," said Sarah proudly. "It lives in the mangroves. You want to see?"

Without waiting for him to answer, Sarah

grabbed her mask, snorkel and fins. Her grandfather took his equipment out of the boat, and within minutes he had joined Sarah, who was already heading across the cove.

Sarah slowed down as she reached the mangroves. Her grandfather caught up to her. They swam slowly side by side along the bank of roots.

Granddad pointed out fish and crabs of all kinds as they passed. Sarah looked deep into the maze for just one thing—the shark. Finally she recognized the now-familiar shape. It was barely visible. She signaled for her grandfather to stop and waited for his eyes to focus on what she had found. He nodded his head up and down when he saw the shark and then lifted his head out of the water.

"You're right!" he exclaimed after he removed his snorkel. "It's the lemon shark. It must have been born here, on these flats, with ten to fifteen other pups. They'll live in these mangroves for several years until they're big enough to survive in the open water."

"Where are its brothers and sisters?" Sarah asked.

"The ones that are still alive are hidden all

around here. It's not easy to find them. Only about half of these pups will live through their first year. Only a very few of those will live to become adults. And only a tiny fraction of those will live to old age. It's not easy to be a shark."

"What about their mother?" Sarah asked, with just the slightest tingle up her back as she looked out into the deeper water.

"She gives birth and then goes back to deeper water. If she survives, she'll return in two years and deliver more pups. It's possible she could live to be as old as I am." He smiled at the astonished look on Sarah's face.

"Possible, but not likely," her grandfather admitted. "There should be some other shark pups around here. Little nurse sharks and tiger sharks live in these mangroves, too." He ducked his head underwater and then burst back up again.

"Look, there's a mosquito fish!" he cried. "They eat the tiny mosquito larvae before they become pests!" He plunged back under the water. Sarah just shook her head and smiled. She adjusted her mask and snorkel and followed her grandfather around the bend.

5
▼▼▼

Swimming with Sharks

A week later Sarah woke up before dawn, as she did regularly now. She eagerly greeted her grandfather in the hallway.

"Granddad," she pleaded, "I've *got* to go out with you this morning and check the lines. I'm sure you caught something."

"Well, well, you are, are you?" Granddad replied with a wry smile. "You'd be worth millions to the fishing industry if you sold your talents."

"Seriously, Granddad," Sarah pressed, "I'll help you get ready and you can stay out all day. And if we don't find a shark I won't complain, I promise."

Her grandfather rubbed the rough stubble on his chin. "I know you. You won't let me come home until you see a shark! Remember, I'm an old man and I've got to get my rest."

"Oh, foo," said Sarah quickly, "you're no older than I am inside. I can go, can't I?"

"Yes, you *may* go."

Without a word, Sarah darted off to her room to get changed. Her grandfather watched her go with a lift of his eyebrows and a nod of his head. Sarah was "shark crazy." She followed him around asking questions about sharks. She begged him to take her out to see big sharks. She really wasn't very different from his students.

He walked into the kitchen and poured himself a cup of coffee. Edie was sitting at the table. Long ago she had gotten used to waking up early with her husband, and the habit had stuck.

"Good morning, Joe," she piped from the other side of the kitchen, where she was watching the dawn brighten the five-A.M. sky.

"And a good morning it is," answered Joe. At seventy, Edie had white hair and a weathered face, and eyes that glowed with a keen interest in all that went on around her.

29

"Looks like our granddaughter has caught the bug," said Joe with a twinkle in his eye. "I'd like to take her out for a shark swim. What do you think?"

"Apparently she's been swimming with sharks all summer," Edie teased. "But seriously, Joe, wait and see how she feels when she sees a big shark. That's a very different experience."

At that moment Sarah flew into the room and the conversation stopped.

"I'm ready, Granddad," said Sarah, adding in the same breath, "let's go."

"Hold on, young lady. We have to eat breakfast, cut bait and pack the boat. We'll get there, I promise. But we have a few things to do before we can leave."

"Good morning, sweet sunshine," chimed Grandma. "Go help your grandfather get ready while I fix breakfast and pack you a lunch. I have a feeling you'll be gone most of the day."

An hour later they were in the boat.

"Take in those lines," Granddad ordered as he readied the boat. Sarah removed the ropes from the pilings; then Granddad put the boat in reverse and pulled away from the dock.

"Come on back now and sit with me," Granddad called. Sarah perched on the chair next to her grandfather behind the windscreen. She jammed her hat down on her head. She knew from past experience that Granddad drove at two speeds: very slow or very fast. They moved slowly out of the inlet.

"Ready?" called Granddad.

"Ready!" cried Sarah. Granddad pulled down on the throttle and the boat surged forward. It sped across the dappled blue water and out toward the reef. The bay was choppy. Every wave lifted the bow and then slammed it down again as it passed. Sarah squealed with delight.

When they found the bright red buoy that marked Granddad's fishing line, they slowed to a crawl. Sarah watched as her grandfather cut the engines and reached for the heavy wire cable that stretched between the red buoys. Hand over hand he brought the cable up, checking the hooks that hung down on long wires every twenty feet.

One hook came up empty. The bait was gone. Sarah reached into the chum bucket to get another piece for her grandfather. The mixture of old fish, blood and leftover meat scraps looked awful and smelled worse. For a moment Sarah felt as if she might get sick.

"Can't take it?" Granddad teased. Sarah flashed him an angry look and reached into the bucket and handed him a piece of fish. "That's more like it," he said approvingly. Then she quickly dipped her hands into the clean, salty water alongside the boat.

They continued in silence until a huge shadow became visible at the end of the next line. Immediately Sarah's grandfather was alert.

"Grab the anchor, Sarah," Granddad ordered.

Sarah picked up the anchor with two hands. It swung back and forth with the rocking of the boat and knocked her in the knee.

"Ow," muttered Sarah. "Where do you want me to throw this thing?"

"Throw it out on the other side of the boat, then give it a pull to set it. Make sure it's set well!"

The fish was still as Sarah set the anchor. Her chore done, Sarah leaned over to take a peek.

"Oh, my . . ." Sarah began, and then fell silent. Before her was the biggest shark she had ever seen or even imagined seeing.

"Now, go over and grab onto that chair," warned Granddad. "It's a tiger shark. A big one. I'm going to pull it in and tie it to the front of the boat, then rope its tail. Once I've lashed it to the boat, you can come over to this side. I don't know how long it's been hooked. If it's been here awhile, it'll be a puppy—if not, we'll have a good fight on our hands!"

Sarah gripped the chair while her grandfather hauled in the shark. She shuddered to think how easily the big tiger shark could overpower him. She guessed it was almost twice as long as he was. That would be at least eleven feet! She held her breath as he strained to bring up the line and fasten it to the front of the boat.

Suddenly the tiger shark came alive. It twisted and rolled. Sarah tightened her arms around the back of the chair. Her grandfather strained to keep hold of the thick wire that held the shark. He managed to wind it around the cleat on the side of the boat. The boat lurched violently. The thrashing shark yanked the side of the boat dangerously close to the waterline with each roll. Sarah screamed. Then all was still. Gripping the railing, Granddad made his way toward the great fish's tail. With a sureness that was the result of decades of experience, he made a loop with the line and in one quick movement had the tail of the tiger shark secured to the boat.

"Come take a look," Granddad said. "It's a male. See those two tubes? They're called claspers. Females don't have them." He reached out and held her arm as she made her way toward the side of the boat. "Once he's on his back, he can't move. It's a normal response. It's as if he were hypnotized. This fellow weighs at least eleven hundred pounds. That's a lot of fish."

Sarah moved cautiously. When she looked over the railing, she saw the massive form of the tiger shark. His belly was pale, his back dark. Sarah watched the great fish in awe. He was tremendous. Compared to her sleek little lemon shark, this animal was broad and block-like. He made the boat feel small. She held on to the side rail tightly.

"Hold on," ordered Granddad. "I want to take some pictures." Sarah nodded and waited

nervously while her grandfather focused his attention on his camera. She watched as he leaned over the railing to take close-ups of the shark's teeth and tail.

The tiger shark's teeth were just what Sarah had imagined. They were sharp, jagged and hooked. On closer inspection she could see they were shaped like a rooster's comb. She could see several rows of new teeth erupting out of the gums. She knew from her grandfather that most sharks had five rows of teeth ready to move in to replace those that were worn or lost. She also knew this endless supply of razor-sharp teeth was just *one* of the reasons sharks were such successful predators.

The big, fearsome fish was still. Sarah relaxed her grip a bit. She could see that the tiger shark's back was mottled with gray and black spots that formed stripes like his namesake, the tiger. His eye was large and dark.

There was a majesty about this animal. Sarah had the feeling he had lived many years and seen many things. His black eye seemed to look into her, not just at her. For a moment she longed to reach out and touch the big shark, but she glanced at his teeth again and thought better of that idea.

"Granddad," called Sarah, "can we let him go now? This is enough. He needs to be free."

Joe Santos smiled at his granddaughter. She didn't know all that he had planned for that day.

"Sure," he said, and put down his camera. "How would you like to get in the water with me and watch him leave after I release him?"

Sarah stared at her grandfather. Her eyes were as large as the tiger shark's.

"Get in the water?" she stammered. "With this shark? This is a tiger shark. Isn't this a *very dangerous* shark? Look at those teeth!" She paused as she noticed the look in her grandfather's eyes. He was serious. Here was the man in the family stories. The man who swam with sharks. In her wildest dreams, however, she had never thought he would let *her* swim with them!

"You're serious, aren't you?" Sarah asked. "What will happen?"

"If we're lucky, he'll stay around long enough for us to get in and watch him leave." He watched his granddaughter closely. Joe Santos had been swimming with sharks for many years as part of his work. He had never felt he was in any danger. But he was no fool and knew there were always risks when you were near any wild animal. And sharks were not just "any animal."

Sarah looked carefully at the shark again. She knew from her grandfather that the stories about sharks as killers who ate anything in their path were wrong. She knew it, but she wasn't sure she really believed it.

Sarah felt so . . . bare and . . . unprotected next to the shark with all his senses, his knifelike teeth and his rough, thick skin. Then again, this was a chance to get closer to a tiger shark than almost any other person in the entire world! And he was a big tiger shark at that! She looked at her grandfather. He knew more than anyone about sharks. He would never put her in danger. Well, not *dangerous* danger.

"I'll get ready," said Sarah, scared but determined. "I have my snorkeling things in my bag." Her grandfather flashed her another rare smile. Immediately he was back to business.

"This is what we'll do," he said in his matter-of-fact voice. "I'll take out the hook. Then I'll release the rope on his tail and get in the water. You slip off the back of the boat behind me. If the shark comes toward us, just stay calm and don't wave your hands or feet in front of him. He's tired now and won't bother us if we move slowly. It's perfectly natural for you to be scared. You need to pay attention to those feelings. If you feel you need to get out, slowly take off your flippers and use the step on the back of the boat. I'll help you. It's better to leave than to panic. All set?"

"Yes, Granddad," Sarah croaked. She was excited and scared. Her insides felt queasy.

He released the shark and slid after it into the water. Still aboard the boat, Sarah was shaking. Her arms and legs felt weak. As she looked at the water, her teeth started to chatter. Sarah thought about all the times she had worried about sharks when she dove off a boat or through a wave. Now she *knew* a shark was below her. A big shark. The kind of shark that many people called a "floating garbage pit" because it could eat almost anything—nails, boards, people, you name it.

Sarah shook her head and looked down. Granddad was in the water and the "garbage pit" hadn't eaten him.

"Come now or he'll be gone," her grandfather urged quietly.

Sarah was ready. She slipped off the back of the boat behind him. All of her experience swimming in the bay paid off—she hardly made a ripple. Reaching out, she grabbed her grandfather's hand. They floated on the ocean surface, bobbing up and down in the waves.

The tiger shark rested on the bottom not ten feet from them. In an effort to forget how scared she was, Sarah tried to imagine how it would feel to be the shark. The lateral lines that ran down her sides would feel pressure and vibrations around her—like reaching out with long, invisible hands. She would feel the two people above. She would feel the boat and the reef ahead of her. She would see clearly the world around her. She would smell the scents of the sea and perhaps wonder in some sharklike way at the scent of the humans above her. She would hear the waves slapping against the boat

and the fish nibbling on the coral.

Sarah watched as the shark's gills pumped and his eyes focused. His specialized pores tuned in to the Earth's magnetic fields. The big tiger shark took in all the information he could using each of his senses. Then he located himself on the planet and slowly moved toward deeper water.

Sarah was no longer scared. The shark's behavior hadn't frightened her. When her grandfather signaled that they should follow the shark, she swam forward fearlessly.

After a few minutes the shark's movements quickened. Sarah and her grandfather stopped at a respectful distance. An instant later the giant that had seemed to fill the sea was gone. He had vanished. There was nothing left but the brilliant blue water of Florida Bay as far as they could see.

6
▼▼▼

Shark
Classes

"Teach me more about sharks," Sarah pleaded at the dinner table.

"Here now, young lady," said her grandfather playfully, "I've taught you all I know."

"No you haven't," Sarah insisted. "Teach me like you used to teach your classes."

Sarah's grandmother watched the two people at the table with her. Sarah's mother had been right. Sarah, it turned out, was just what her husband needed to help him adjust to retirement. Though now it sounded like she wouldn't allow him to retire after all.

"I don't have any children's books on sharks,"

Sarah's grandfather protested. "All I have are scientific papers and stacks of books that are probably too difficult for you to understand."

"Let me try," Sarah begged. "I can read anything I want. I've already read the two big books about sharks on the coffee table. Besides, you can explain them to me. We'll have classes just like college!"

"Okay, then," Granddad agreed. "We can give it a try if you promise to work hard."

"I will, I will!" Sarah shouted. "Let's start tonight!"

"Tonight?" moaned her grandfather. "I have to dig up my materials and plan my talks. I'll tell you what. I'll give you a few important facts tonight and then we'll start the real work tomorrow. How's that?"

Sarah beamed. "Okay. What facts?"

"Just a few basics," began Granddad in his college lecturing voice. "Sharks belong to a large group of fish that do not have bones. Their skeletons are made of cartilage—the same material your ears are made of."

Sarah reached for her ear. "Really?"

"Really. Depending on how you look at it—

and believe me, scientists can look at it a lot of different ways—there are between eight hundred and a thousand types of cartilaginous fish. About three hundred and seventy of these are sharks.

"There are many different kinds of sharks. Tiny ones like the dwarf shark grow to be only ten inches long. Huge ones like the whale shark grow to be forty-five feet but eat only plankton, the smallest plants and animals in the ocean. And then there's the famous white shark, which eats very large prey such as seals and other marine mammals.

"People often think of sharks as primitive creatures," Granddad continued. "Actually, many sharks are highly evolved." At this, Grandma slipped away from the table. Joe was hitting his professorial stride and this lecture might go on for quite a while.

"They've existed on the Earth almost four hundred million years. They have highly developed senses. Their sight is excellent, especially in dim underwater light. Their sense of smell is good, too. Their noses use water instead of air. They can smell the tiniest bits of blood and tissue in their environment. To track their prey, they swing their heads back and forth, which fills each nostril with water. They just follow the current right to the source. Their hearing is superb, especially in the low frequencies. For instance, they can hear the sounds of a fish struggling, a splash or even a helicopter.

"Sharks also have more senses than we do. Like all fish, they have two cords called lateral lines that run down each side. The cells in these lines detect vibrations or pressure changes in the water. They help the shark feel its way through the ocean, which can be a very difficult place to see."

Sarah thought about earlier in the day, when she had pretended to be the tiger shark.

"And . . . then there are the ampullae of Lorenzini." He said the name slowly, with great drama. Sarah perked up and listened carefully.

"'Ampullae' means vials, and Lorenzini was the scientist who discovered them way back in 1678. Can you say it?"

"Am-*pu*-lay of Lorenzini," repeated Sarah promptly.

"The ampullae of Lorenzini are very specialized

pores located around the shark's head. We know now that they are very sensitive to electric fields, such as those produced by the nerves in a living organism." Granddad paused. "Did you know that all animals produce tiny electric fields?"

"Yes, Granddad," said Sarah with a wry grin. "I watch TV. There was a program about that last year." She smiled because she knew her grandfather hated TV.

"I suppose that's possible." Granddad gave in. Then he continued. "Lorenzini identified them, but he had no way of knowing how incredible they really were. We know that the ampullae allow sharks to find . . . to feel other living animals close by. Even those that have hidden themselves under the sand for protection! So when sharks are hungry, they are superbly equipped to find their food. Or did you learn that on TV, too?"

"Nope," Sarah admitted, "that's news to me!"

"Good," said Granddad. "Now, contrary to what most people learn on television, sharks don't eat everything they see. If they did, they would not fit into the balance of life in the oceans. Scientists believe that they prefer to eat what is familiar to them, just like you. If I served you a big bowl of delicious insects, you probably wouldn't eat them, unless you were starving. Would you?"

"Not if my life depended on it," Sarah replied.

"And just like yours," Granddad continued, "sharks' tastes tend toward the things they're used to eating. Though it's true that some sharks are less discriminating than others. A white shark, for instance, lives in the open ocean. There is more water than food out there. So when the white shark comes inshore looking for a nice, juicy seal to eat, and it comes across something very much like a seal—a surfer in a wet suit, for instance—it often bites first and *then* makes the decision whether to finish the meal or not . . . which isn't so great if you're the surfer."

Sarah smiled and nodded. "It's kind of like catch-and-release fishing only it's the fish doing the catching!"

"Exactly!" Granddad agreed. "If sharks were as bad as the movies made them out to be," he continued, "no one would ever be able to set foot in the water, because sharks are everywhere. They are an important part of the sea—and they are very well adapted to find their food or anything else they might want. But they aren't the killers we've been taught to believe. And we need them. We need them because we need a healthy ocean, and we need them for things we might not even realize yet. For example, did you know that sharks rarely get cancer?"

"Really?" asked Sarah, eyes wide. "Why not?"

"We don't know. We only know it has something to do with their immune system," said Sarah's grandfather. "But wouldn't it be nice to find out why before we erase them from the Earth?"

Sarah nodded.

"Now eat up," ordered Granddad, pointing to Sarah's dinner. "We've got some busy days ahead of us."

7

▼▼▼

Tracking
a Shark

The next morning they began a routine that would continue for the rest of the summer. Edie, Joe and then Sarah woke up early. Sarah drank a big cup of dark, homemade hot chocolate. Joe and Edie drank their Cuban coffee. The scent of the coffee beans became pleasing to Sarah. It meant the start of a great day.

Sarah made a list of the things she needed to do every morning to help her grandfather prepare for a day on the water.

- Clean anchor lines and check for weak spots
- Make sure there are three anchors on board

- Check fuel tank levels
- Check life preservers
- Fill water bottles
- Get yummy picnic lunch from Grandma

She whisked through her duties and grabbed her backpack, now filled with snorkeling gear, sunscreen, sunglasses, a hat, a big shirt, a pencil and notebook, a bottle of water and one of Granddad's shark papers.

When her grandfather had finished tinkering with the engine, he and Sarah would set off to find sharks.

One day Sarah's grandfather arranged for them to track a large female lemon shark.

"Put on this headset, Sarah," he said as he handed her a set of large, padded earphones, "and hold this tube." He handed Sarah a white, plastic pipe shaped like an upside-down L. "It's attached to an underwater microphone called a hydrophone. This box over here is called a receiver. It picks up the sound from the shark's tag through the hydrophone and then sends it to your earphones." Sarah was amazed at all the equipment they needed to find a single shark.

"All you do is move the tube slowly back and forth, from one side to the other, until you hear a *ping*. The direction the tube is facing when the *ping* is loudest is the direction we need to go to find the shark. Simple!" Sarah squinted up at her grandfather. Without a comment, she turned and swept the hydrophone in a big arc. Sarah listened closely. She didn't hear anything that sounded like a *ping*. Her eyebrows rose questioningly as she turned to her grandfather.

"Don't worry. Sometimes it takes a long time before you hear anything," he reassured her. They launched the boat and made their way slowly out of the channel.

Sarah held on to the seat next to her grandfather as they threaded their way among the tree islands and creeks to the open sea. The boat skimmed over the open water. Sarah watched carefully and picked out the shadows of stingrays and sea turtles as they sped by.

"There's a big stingray!" shouted Sarah over the roar of the engines.

"Yes!" Sarah's grandfather shouted back. "There seem to be more of them now. It may be because sharks are becoming so rare. Sharks feed on stingrays. Less sharks mean more stingrays. So it's not necessarily a good sign, sharkwise." Sarah nodded and continued to watch the water.

After a while Granddad stopped the boat, and Sarah adjusted her earphones. She picked up the tracking tube and dropped the hydrophone in the water. She began to move the instrument slowly back and forth across the horizon.

At first the tracking was exciting, and the possibility of finding a shark at any minute kept Sarah on edge. Then, as the minutes stretched into hours, it became annoying, then disappointing, then downright boring. The sun was fierce. It seemed even hotter because they weren't going as fast as usual. Sarah swept the pipe back and forth, back and forth. Her lips and arms began to burn despite the heavy layer of sunscreen she wore.

"Granddad," Sarah called, "how long do you think this will take?"

"Depends," said Granddad.

Oh, great, thought Sarah, and readjusted her headphones.

Three hours later they were still looking for their shark. They had moved up and down the bay. Sarah was discouraged, hot and tired.

"This is what it's like," said Granddad and patted her head. "All the wonderful things we've learned about sharks are backed up by many, many long, difficult hours of research. Sooner or later we'll find something. I'll head out into deeper water. Often sharks go offshore during the day, then come back in the evening."

They ate lunch, read from a shark paper and watched for turtles. Sarah took turns steering the boat when she wasn't listening for *ping*s. They traded back and forth. It was Sarah's turn to listen again. She scanned with the tube. Nothing. Then, just as she was about to give up and beg to be taken back home, she heard something.

"Granddad!" she shouted. "I hear a *ping*! I think. Wait. No. Yes. Yes. Yes!" Sarah turned the pipe and pointed in the direction the sound was loudest. Granddad steered the boat in that direction. She lost the sound and then found it again. This time it was headed toward shore. They followed.

The heat of the sun and the wait were forgotten. Sarah had found a shark—a shark that they could never have found without the tiny transmitter attached to its dorsal fin. Now they could track its movements and find out what it was doing on a sunny day in July. The *ping*s became louder as they moved toward a shallow, sandy area.

"Sarah, look there," Granddad called. Ahead of them was a dark, cigar-shaped shadow with two pectoral fins on each side and two dorsal fins almost the same size on its back. Sarah squealed. It looked just like her shark, only bigger.

"Judging from her size," said Granddad, "she could be the mother of your little shark. She's old enough and she's in the right area. She'll stay out here, along the coast, for another month or so." Sarah looked out at the rippling shadow ahead of them. She thought about her small shark darting in and out of the mangroves.

"Granddad, how long will it take my shark to get as big as she is?" Sarah asked.

"At least twelve years, probably more," said Granddad. "Sharks grow ver-r-ry slowly. That's one of the reasons why we need to protect them. It will take a long time to replace the sharks that have disappeared."

The female lemon shark had no way of knowing she was electronically linked to the humans in the boat. She came to a halt. The boat stopped, too. She began moving again. The boat followed. They halted and moved and spent the rest of the afternoon crossing the bay at the shark's pace.

Finally thunderheads began to gather and Granddad turned toward home.

That night they read an article written by a scientist who had tracked young lemon sharks using the same method as Sarah and her grandfather. He determined that the younger sharks, like Sarah's pup, stayed close to the mangroves for several years, probably to avoid being eaten by larger fish and other sharks.

"Eaten by sharks?" exclaimed Sarah. "That's terrible! Why would they eat each other?"

"We don't know the real reason," answered Granddad. "Perhaps there is some genetic benefit, or perhaps they just happen to be the right size. We don't know. You have to stop judging an animal from our point of view. Animals aren't good or evil, they just do certain things. As scientists, we observe what they do and try to understand them. Understanding them is much harder to do than it sounds. It would be easy to say the lemon shark we saw today was out on the reef having a nice time. But was she? We only know that she was moving from place to place. She wasn't in a hurry. She didn't eat. She moved from deep water to shallow water as the day progressed. But we don't know the true shark reason she did all these things."

"When will we know?" Sarah asked.

"When you grow up," Granddad said seriously, "and computers and transmitters track and transmit information about many sharks over their entire lifetimes. Even then we still may not know everything or really be able to understand what it's like to think with their brains."

"Good. I wouldn't want us to know *all* their secrets. How much danger are sharks in now?" Sarah asked.

"Grave danger. Many kinds of sharks are endangered and could become extinct very quickly. Many shark populations have dropped since the seventies. We kill at least thirty million sharks every year. And some people think it's as many as one hundred million. Lemon sharks must be twelve or thirteen years old before they can have pups, and other species of sharks must be even older. Plus sharks have only a few babies at a time compared with other fish, which spew out millions and millions of eggs each year. We need to act quickly if we want to save sharks."

Sarah nodded. The math was simple.

8
▼▼▼

Sharks
All Around

The rain poured down. Sarah could hear the water gurgling down the gutter pipes. An unusually wet and lingering storm had kept Sarah and her grandparents inside for several days. Sarah's grandfather gave her a stack of books so she could compare the chance of being eaten by a shark with other dangers.

"Every year about ten people in the United States are killed by sharks," her grandfather told Sarah. "Make a list of things you find that are more dangerous."

Sarah worked for a while.

"What does 1:300,000,000 mean?"

"That means one chance in three hundred million," said her grandfather. "Why?"

"Well, that's your chance of being killed by a shark, according to this almanac," Sarah said. Then she started to laugh. "You have a one in ten million chance of being killed by a falling airplane part, a one in five and a half million chance of being killed by a bee, and a one in six thousand chance of being killed playing soccer in England. And look here, you have a better chance of being killed by a *pig* than a shark!" The thought of being terrified of a pig suddenly seemed so funny that Sarah fell over laughing. Soon her grandparents were laughing as well.

"I can see it now," said Sarah, barely able to get her breath. "*Snouts*! Coming soon to a theater near you!"

When she finally stopped laughing, Grandma said, "I hear it's going to be nice tomorrow. Why don't we all go out to the reef, Joe? There's that beautiful spot where we usually see Caribbean reef sharks and blacktips, and we might even see a hammerhead. I hardly get to see my granddaughter now that you've started this shark business. I guess I'll have to join you."

"You swim with sharks, too?" asked Sarah, amazed.

"I couldn't be married to your grandfather for over fifty years and not swim with sharks!" said Sarah's grandmother with a big smile.

"What about Mom?" asked Sarah. "Did she swim with sharks?"

"Your mom, too," Grandma admitted. "Though she was afraid of sharks until she was much older than you. She used to worry about your grandfather being eaten. It was a different time. Very few people understood sharks the way your grandfather did, and they scared her with their stories."

The next day dawned with clear skies as promised. A gentle breeze was the only thing that stirred the water.

Sarah ran out to feed her lemon shark and the other fish that lived around the dock. She watched as the lemon shark appeared on schedule.

"Granddad says that scientists have studied sharks like you," Sarah told the shark as she fed it. "He says you can learn how to get through a maze faster than a cat!" Suddenly she remembered all they had planned for the day. She ran to do her morning chores.

By nine the boat was packed and they were ready to go. The boat's bow broke the perfect, glassy surface of the water.

"Better hang on, Grandma," warned Sarah. "As soon as we get around the bend, Granddad will step on it."

"I know," said Grandma, and laughed. "He's been driving that way since I can remember."

They bounced across the bay to a place Sarah's grandparents seemed to know by heart. As always, Granddad anchored carefully in the sand so he wouldn't damage the coral. As Grandma and Sarah put on their masks, snorkels and fins, Granddad gleefully threw stinky clumps of chum overboard.

"Hold on to the anchor rope and stay with Grandma," Granddad called. "Don't raise your hands or swim away from the boat. These sharks will be using their senses of smell and sight to find the fish. They'll know the difference between you and a piece of chum." As he spoke these words of caution, he watched the water carefully.

Sarah's stomach tightened. Even though she had done this before, it was still scary. For an instant she almost lost her nerve. Panicked, she looked over at her grandfather. He was so happy throwing those smelly hunks of fish and meat into the water! Her grandmother slipped off the boat. Sarah took a deep breath and slowly let it out. That made her feel calmer. She crossed her fingers and slid into the water.

Her grandmother watched as Sarah entered the water. She waved her over to the anchor line and then pointed to a large barracuda. Sarah had watched barracuda for years, and the sight of their needle-sharp teeth did not bother her. She had bigger teeth to worry about.

She didn't have to wait long before a distinctive shape emerged from around the coral island. Then another. Within minutes six sharks ranging from five to eight feet long had appeared. They fed on the bits of chum. The reef fish didn't leave; they were also feeding on the tiny bits of fish in the water. Sarah had always thought that all the fish in the area fled when sharks arrived—another myth. The sharks and fish swam and turned together in a swirling, ever-changing mass. More sharks arrived. Soon there were almost a dozen in front of them. Grandma spoke through her snorkel.

"These are all Caribbean reef sharks." Grandma's words were a bit garbled but Sarah could understand her. "This large one is a female. See the others over there? They have claspers attached to their pelvic fins—the fins on their bellies. They're males."

Sarah nodded. She'd seen claspers on the tiger shark.

"The claspers were named by Aristotle, who thought the male sharks grabbed the females with them. The name stuck even though we now know they don't grab with them."

"What do they do with them?" asked Sarah, suddenly curious.

"They mate," answered Grandma. Her eyes crinkled behind her mask.

"Oh-h," said Sarah and then quickly tuned in to what was happening around them.

The activity had picked up and the sharks were moving more quickly. One passed within two feet of Sarah and Edie. Sarah squealed through her snorkel as the shark retreated into the deep, hazy blueness beyond their sight. She held on to the rope as several smaller sharks arrived.

"That's a nurse shark," Grandma sputtered and pointed to a small shark near the bottom. "See how its mouth is nearly at the end—not underneath like the other sharks. Look, there! That's a blacktip shark. And over there's a little sharpnose shark! They never get much bigger than three feet long."

Sharks were everywhere. They moved swiftly at times and slowly at others. It seemed to Sarah that they were aware of each other and of the humans as well. Granddad eased into the water after throwing out the last of the chum. At the sound of his splash the sharks departed to the edges of the white sand clearing. When he moved to the anchor line, they returned. A cloud of blood dissolved into the water.

"Why don't they eat the other fish?" Sarah

asked as clearly as she could through her snorkel.

"It's too much work," hooted Granddad. "They'd rather get an easy meal of chum than use up energy chasing a fish they might not catch." That seemed sensible, Sarah thought.

"Look here," Granddad called as he pointed out a small blue fish with a black-and-white striped head. "That's a wrasse. They're 'cleaner fish.' They eat parasites, tiny animals that make their homes in the sharks' skin and gills. See that big angelfish tilt sideways! That's a signal that the wrasse may approach and 'clean' it." Sarah watched the fish nibble for a moment and then move on to the head of a shark. The shark wasn't bothered, and the fish soon ate its fill and left.

An odd-looking fish with a flat place on its head that looked like the sole of a running shoe swam by.

Sarah pointed to it, and Grandma called out, "A remora! I love them. They attach themselves to bigger animals and get a free ride." The remora swam under the bank of humans holding on to the rope.

"I think it wants to come with *us*." Sarah huffed and giggled.

Sarah was amazed that she could be so relaxed with sharks all around her. They were perfectly adapted to the reef and the ocean. It made the three humans seem very unimportant. The sharks and the fish danced in a ballet that they'd perfected over the eons they had existed in the sea.

The chum was soon gone and so were the sharks. Sarah wondered how far the sharks had come and where they had all gone. She thought of the lemon shark they'd tracked and her times of activity and times of stillness.

The reef fish schooled and spun in one large group. There was no sign that a dozen sharks had just fed among them. The soft pulses of the waves moved the entire community of plants and animals. The light played through the water streaking down in columns. It was just another moment in time on the reef. It could have been any moment in the past hundreds of millions of years. But this moment was Sarah's.

The reef cast its spell on the group. Sarah swam out, held her breath and dove to get a better look at the corals. She moved smoothly and gracefully. Her grandfather joined her. Her grandmother chased a school of silvery sardines, with her hair of the same color streaming out behind her. Sarah dove after her grandfather to inspect the lobsters, crabs and small fish he pointed out.

On one dive he found a sleeping nurse shark wedged beneath a coral head. Sarah dove down and hung there as long as she could before she had to return to the surface for another breath.

As the humans scrambled back into their boat, the spell was broken. They were no longer creatures of the reef. They dried off, opened the cooler and took out their lunch.

"So what do you think your friends are doing right now?" asked Grandma.

"Nothing like this," Sarah replied, and took a huge bite of her ham sandwich. Joe Santos looked out over the turquoise water where the sharks had just been feeding and quietly nodded his head.

9
▼▼▼

The Top
Predator

The days of research and study continued for
Sarah and Granddad. Each day flowed into
the next, interrupted only by rainy days, trips
to the library and cooking sessions with
Grandma. Sarah spoke to her parents every
week on the phone. She chatted happily about
her adventures. The summer was turning out
better than she had ever dreamed.

Sarah no longer needed the checklist. She
knew exactly what she had to do each morning.
Sometimes Grandma would come with them.
Other days she would stay home to help "my
ladies," as she called the women she counseled.

Besides teaching them English, she helped them find apartments, get car loans and do all kinds of things Sarah had never thought about before this summer. Grandma worked mainly on the phone, but occasionally she went out to take someone to the bank for the first time or help her apply for a job. Today she was needed on the phone.

Sarah put the picnic cooler in the boat. She opened the lid and broke off a piece of bread. She crumbled it in her hands, then leaned over the water and sprinkled crumbs on the surface. The "regulars" appeared. She fed them carefully and waited for the lemon shark. Sure enough, it arrived to eat as usual. Sarah reached into the chum bucket for a piece of fish. The shark ate its fill and left. She rinsed her hand in the warm, clear water. When she heard her grandfather close the door, she got up.

"'Bye, Edie," he called. "We're off!"

Sarah heard a muffled reply and he joined her on the dock.

"Ready?" he asked.

"Ready," said Sarah. "What are we doing today?"

"I thought we would try something different," said Granddad. "The weather looks good and the tide is right. I thought we might go out to an area where I almost always see hammerheads."

"Hammerheads!" cried Sarah. "They're the best, the ultimate, the . . . Let's go!"

It took about an hour for them to reach the site.

As they approached, they saw what looked like a large sportfishing boat.

"Shoot," grumbled Granddad. That was as close to swearing as he would get in front of Sarah, though Sarah had no doubt he could let loose a colorful stream of words and phrases if he chose. "Looks like we have company. Big charter boat." He picked up his binoculars.

"That's odd," he mumbled, and looked again.

"What's the matter, Granddad?" Sarah asked. The longer he watched the big yacht, the more worried he seemed.

"That's him, all right," Granddad said, scowling. "I wondered what had happened to him the last few years. I thought he had gone to Australia to do his dirty work there."

"Who went to Australia?" asked Sarah.

"The boat up ahead belongs to a man who takes very rich clients shark fishing. He usually targets areas where there has just been a shark attack. He feeds on the fear of the local people by promising to wipe out the 'man-killers.' More often than not, the 'man-killers' he hunts aren't even the same species that were involved in the attack. People know so little about sharks, they can't tell the difference. He's responsible for killing thousands of large sharks."

"Can't you have him arrested or something?" pleaded Sarah.

"We could if we could catch him again. Now there are laws protecting sharks. But most people are afraid of sharks and don't care if other people kill them."

"Look, Granddad, he's leaving. Should we follow him?" asked Sarah.

"No," said Sarah's grandfather, and then paused to think. "It's strange that he doesn't have any customers. I wonder if he has a finning operation going."

"Finning?" asked Sarah.

"Let's go see what they were after," said Granddad. Sarah decided to wait before she asked him any more questions.

"I must warn you, Sarah—if this is a finning operation, what we find might be very upsetting. First they cut all the fins off the shark. Then the sharks are thrown back to become bait for other sharks or to die a long, terrible death."

Sarah gasped. Her grandfather patted her back.

"What do they do with the fins?" asked Sarah.

"Usually they freeze or dry them so they can store them. Then they sell them to make a highly prized dish called shark-fin soup."

"Oh," said Sarah. That was more than she really wanted to know. They rode the rest of the way in silence.

"Get the anchor ready," shouted Granddad. Sarah was thankful for something to do. Her arms shook as she pulled the anchor out of the hatch and threw it overboard. Everything looked normal, she told herself.

After the boat was secured, Sarah's grandfather got out his underwater camera and snorkeling gear.

"I'll go in first," he said. "Then, if every-thing is all right, you can come in." Sarah's lips were set in a straight line, her brow creased. Granddad slipped over the side. He adjusted his mask and kicked away from the boat with his underwater camera cradled in his arm. He looked very far away to Sarah. Suddenly, with a kick, he was gone. Sarah knew that he was just diving down to get a closer look at something. It was what he might see that bothered her. She felt very much alone.

Then, with a burst of air and water, he sur-faced. He headed back toward the boat.

"I think we must've interrupted them!" Sarah's grandfather called. "There's only one hammerhead down there. He had been finned and was still alive. There was nothing I could do for him, so I put him out of his misery."

"How did you do that?" asked Sarah inno-cently.

"It sounds terrible, but I cut the nerve at the base of its head with my knife. The shark died immediately. We're lucky—there might have been more."

"Can I see it?" Sarah asked.

"It's a sad sight," warned her grandfather.

Suddenly Sarah had an idea. "Granddad, couldn't you take a picture and write a newspaper article about this?"

"Even better," said Granddad, "you write the article. You know more than most people about sharks, young lady. Besides, a kid writing the story might get more sympathy for the sharks."

"I'll do it," said Sarah. "Hold on, I'm coming in."

Sarah struggled with her mask, flippers and snorkel and got into the water. She looked down. Below her lay a great hammerhead. The sight that should have thrilled her shocked her instead. Its dorsal fin, two pectoral fins and pelvic tail fins were missing. The shark lay motionless on the seafloor. She thought about the incredible sensitivity of these animals. There lay a creature so attuned to its environment that it could sense the presence of other life beneath the surface of the sand. It could feel the Earth's magnetic field; it could see, smell and hear the things it needed to much better than she could. And it had been left to die with all its senses intact, and no way to help itself.

Sarah took a deep breath and dove down. Gently she laid her hand on the shark's head. She looked up at her grandfather. Seeing the care in her gesture, he snapped her picture. Then she kicked her flippers and surged to the surface for a breath.

"I've seen enough," Sarah said. "Let's go home."

Her grandfather nodded and they climbed back in the boat.

As they pulled in to the dock, Sarah asked, "How can we keep them from killing more sharks?" She reached for the rope to tie the boat.

"Before I retired," said Granddad, "there were a lot of problems with finners around here. So I organized a group of shark biologists, divers and fishermen, called the Shark Guards. I might be able to get them on the radio. With luck and their help, we might be able to catch these finners before they leave U.S. waters. At least we can watch their every move."

"Why do they do it?" Sarah asked. She could understand catching a few sharks to eat. But just cutting their fins and throwing them back alive? That seemed too cruel.

"Money," he stated. "They get between twenty-five and two hundred dollars a pound for shark fins. I hear shark-fin soup costs around a hundred dollars a bowl in some countries."

Sarah whistled long and low when she realized how much money Granddad was talking about.

"I guess sharks aren't the top predator in the sea, right, Granddad?"

"Not any longer. Oddly, some humans behave much more like the sharks we see in the movies than the sharks themselves."

"I'm going to get to work on my story," said Sarah, and she headed for the house.

10
▼▼▼

The Shark
Guards

Granddad called a meeting of the Shark Guards as soon as he got home. Soon the house, yard and cove became packed with fishermen, divers and scientists.

The first thing Sarah noticed was that people who liked sharks also seemed to like to wear shark T-shirts. She had never seen so many shark T-shirts. There were red, blue, electric-yellow and green shirts. There were cartoon sharks drawn down over large bellies, and sharks circling around wiry bodies. This was a colorful group in many ways, Sarah thought.

Sarah walked up to one man who wore a

flattened, tan cap and a sun-bleached collared shirt. Despite the age of the shirt, he managed to look dressed up. Dapper is what Sarah's mother would have called him.

"May I interview you?" asked Sarah.

The man looked down at her with a grin, showing a set of perfect white teeth.

"Absolutely, young lady." His voice was deep and loud. "And why are you interviewing me?"

"I am writing an article about finning sharks." Sarah spoke firmly.

"You are, are you?" As he spoke, Sarah watched him closely. He seemed like the kind of person you couldn't fool easily.

"I'll tell you a story instead," he offered. "How's that?"

"All right," Sarah said. There was something about the way he spoke that made it hard to argue. "But I really need information," she managed to say. He laughed as she took out her pencil and notebook.

"What's your name?" he asked.

"Sarah Marshall. I'm Dr. Santos' grand-daughter."

"Ah-h-h," said the man. Sarah didn't like it when adults said "ah-h-h" like that. She waited for him to continue.

"In that case, I'll tell you another story," he said. "My name is Bascum Washington. I've known your grandfather for a long time. I used to be in the poaching business. For a price I hunted anything that moved. I didn't pay much attention to the laws that were passed to protect wildlife. I knew where every alligator nested, and I made a lot of money for a while."

"I thought poachers were big, scary men with bad breath," Sarah said quickly and then blushed. Bascum Washington laughed a deep and hearty laugh.

"Well, you are something, aren't you?" he said. "I guess that's what most people think, but that's just another stereotype. Poachers come in all shapes and sizes, just like anyone else. There probably are a few with bad breath, though," he added with a smile.

"How did you get to know Granddad if you were a poacher?" asked Sarah.

"When I met your grandfather, he was working for the Department of Fish and Game. It was his job to arrest guys like me. We met in a remote area of the Everglades. We were both surprised to see another human being that far out in the back country. We talked a little. Guess he realized he'd met someone who knew as much about wildlife as he did. Instead of arresting me for poaching, he hired me to find other poachers. I've been honest ever since. And I thank your grandfather every day for it, too."

Sarah smiled shyly. "He's been teaching me about sharks, and I thank him every day for that! We swam with sharks on the reef not too far from here. The other day we found a hammerhead that was finned. Granddad recognized the boat that did it. That's why he called this meeting."

"He took a bit of a thing like you in the water with a bunch of sharks!" teased Bascum. Sarah stiffened and stood a little straighter. "I'll bet you're just about bait size for one of those big sharks."

"They weren't interested in me," Sarah began, and then smiled impishly, adding, "I guess the man-eating shark's just another stereotype! On the other hand, maybe man-eating sharks only eat men!"

"Touché!" boomed Bascum Washington, and laughed a deep belly laugh. "I stand corrected!"

"Anyway," continued Sarah, getting back to business, "they were interested in eating chum. It's easier, and they were actually a little afraid of us. They would disappear at the least little move. I wasn't scared. Do you know the man Granddad recognized?"

Bascum squinted his eyes and looked down at Sarah. "I think I do. He's very well liked by people who like the adventure of shark fishing and are willing to pay for it. He fins on the side, I've heard, and makes a bundle. Finning's legal everywhere in the world except for a few protected areas in the United States and Canada."

"Why do they come here then?" asked Sarah.

"So many sharks are being killed that they're getting tough to find. The finners are coming here to U.S. waters because we protect our sharks. Odd, isn't it? Look, there's a young lady over there you should talk to. She works for one of the conservation groups. Her name is Sonja."

Sarah realized she had been brushed off, but Sonja looked like a good candidate for information. She walked over to her.

"May I interview you?" asked Sarah as she looked at Sonja's bright red shark T-shirt. Sonja looked down with an amused expression.

"Sure. Who are you, anyway?" Sonja asked.

Sarah smiled. "I'm Sarah Marshall, Dr. Joe Santos' granddaughter. I was with him when he found the hammerhead."

"My name's Sonja. I work for a group that is trying to protect sharks. I saw your picture, the one your grandfather took. You're a brave kid. I wish I had been there," she added quickly.

"I don't think you would have liked it," said Sarah sadly.

"Why do you want to interview me?" asked Sonja, kindly changing the subject. She could see it was upsetting Sarah.

"I'm writing an article about shark finning for the newspaper. I want them to print it, so it has to be good. Mr. Washington said you could tell me more about finning. Do you know who the finners are?"

"Actually," Sonja began in a new, more serious

voice, "I do know who the finners are, but what's important is that people understand how cruel finning is. Leave their names out of it for now. Write what you saw, Sarah."

Sarah thought a minute and asked, "What will happen to the finner if he's caught?" Sarah took out her pencil again.

"Well, at the very least, all his fins would be taken and he would lose quite a lot of money. And depending on which laws are broken, he might go to jail for quite a long time. The trouble is, it's a big ocean. You and your granddad were lucky to catch him the other day. It isn't usually that easy."

"Granddad wanted all of us to follow him until he gave up or got caught. All these people here today could help." Sarah waited for Sonja to answer.

"If we followed him every day, he might get suspicious. Then he'd leave and find another area where no one bothered him. That way there would still be sharks getting killed. We want to stop him."

"What about tagging the boat," Sarah offered, "the way we tag sharks? That way the Shark

Guards could follow him at a distance . . ."
Sarah hesitated, not knowing what the next
step would be.

". . . and then, at just the right moment, we
call the Coast Guard and they catch him in the
act and arrest him!" continued Sonja, excited
by Sarah's idea. "It might just work. But how
do we tag the boat?"

Sarah looked over at Bascum Washington
and then back at Sonja. They smiled at each
other.

"Oh, Bascum . . ." they called in unison.

11
▼▼▼

The
Finner

"I'm getting too old for this," complained Bascum Washington as he struggled into a ragged, stiff wet suit and yanked at the zipper.

"You'll do great," said Sonja, stepping back to admire the older man. "That wet suit takes the years off . . . and the pounds," she whispered to Sarah. "Now where is your scuba gear? Have you had it checked to see that it works?"

"I don't need to have it checked," grumbled Bascum. "I checked it myself. It's old, but it'll do the job, just like me. This shouldn't take me long."

"Now remember to stay on the far side of the boat," Joe reminded him. "We'll create a diversion on the dock so they won't notice any bubbles."

"I'm ready," said Bascum, and flashed one of his wide, white-toothed smiles. "As long as no one runs me over with a powerboat, I'll be fine."

Sarah stood to one side as the adults helped Bascum with his tanks and weight belt. He was going to scuba across the bottom of the small harbor to the big boat. Meanwhile, she was supposed to skateboard down the pier and fall right in front of the shark finner's boat. This way no one would notice Bascum under the water. Then, while Sarah was making a big fuss, Bascum would insert a radio tag in the hull of the shark fisherman's boat.

"Okay, you're on, Sarah," said Bascum as he rolled backward off the boat into the water. He disappeared, and all they could see were the bubbles as he exhaled through his regulator.

"Let's go, Sarah," Sonja called. Sarah grabbed her skateboard and ran after Sonja. They talked and laughed until they got to the pier that held the shark boat. Sarah jumped on her skateboard. She was pretty good at skateboarding. Most of the kids in her neighborhood in Miami had skateboards, in-line skates or both. But Sarah was used to smooth sidewalks. Skateboarding on a wooden pier was a little different.

"Sarah, I can see Bascum's bubbles," Sonja whispered. "Quick, you'd better get down there!"

Sarah kicked off with her foot and hurtled down toward the boat. Two men were sitting on the back of the finning boat. Below them she could make out the words "Slippery Eel." Dumb name, thought Sarah as she got closer.

The skateboard was moving quickly. Sarah was looking for a place to fake her fall when suddenly one wheel caught between the boards of the dock. Instantly Sarah realized she was going too fast to stop herself. She flew off the skateboard and crashed into a stack of crab traps. The accident was short of its mark, but it was stupendous. Traps went flying in every direction. Sonja screamed, realizing that Sarah

couldn't have planned such a fall. Lazy vacationers, resting in their cabins or enjoying the breeze on the decks of their boats, jumped to attention.

"Sarah, Sarah!" yelled her grandfather, who had been waiting farther down the dock.

"Granddad," Sarah cried from under a stack of traps, "I'm under here!" Sarah tried to figure out how badly she was hurt. Her head throbbed and her right side, which had been scrubbed along the wooden dock, was sore. But nothing was broken and she certainly had created a scene. No one would notice Bascum's bubbles now.

"Ahh-h," she screamed again for effect. Panicked, Sonja and her grandfather threw off the traps and bent over her. She winked to let them know she was all right. They both relaxed and winked back.

"Don't move!" shouted Granddad. A crowd was forming. "Sonja, go ask the people on that boat if we can use their phone." Granddad pointed to the finner's boat several slips down from where Sarah had landed. Sonja looked at him closely and raised her eyebrows.

"Go on," he urged.

"Okay," she said, shrugging her shoulders as she walked quickly toward the boat.

"May I use your phone?" Sonja asked the closer of the two men on the large white boat. "A little girl has had an accident."

"Yes, yes, sure," the larger man answered. He was well muscled and tan from his life on the water.

"Steve, get the phone for the lady," he told the other fellow. "Here, let me help you."

"No, that's . . ." Sonja stood helpless as the fisherman jumped onto the dock. Steve handed her the phone as the larger man ran over to Sarah and threw off the rest of the traps. He checked Sarah quickly and expertly for broken bones. He asked her to move her fingers and toes and felt the bump on her head. When he had determined she wasn't in any grave danger, he scooped her up and carried her onto the boat.

"See here," said Sarah's grandfather. "That's quite enough. Put her down."

"Don't worry, mister," reassured the man, "I'm a trained medic. I have a cold pack on the boat. She'll be fine."

Sarah looked desperately at her grandfather. He shrugged, unable to see any way out of the situation. Sarah was carried onto the very boat they were trying to have seized. She wondered if it could be the wrong boat. These men didn't act like the gangsters she had imagined them to be. Maybe they just worked for the man who owned the boat.

The man carried Sarah into the rear cabin and put her down on a king-sized water bed. The boat was larger than it seemed from the outside, and it was expensively decorated. Even Sarah could tell that this wasn't an ordinary fishing boat.

"Well, young lady," the man said after Sarah was comfortably propped up with pillows. "My name is Hector Burke. This is my boat. You've had quite a fall. Would you like something to drink?"

Sarah's eyes widened and she looked up at her grandfather for approval. She hadn't planned to go this far with her diversion. This was the owner of the boat, so he must be the man they were looking for. Right here in front of her!

She didn't know what to say.

"I think she'd like that. My name is Dr. Joe Santos."

"Dr. Joseph Santos?" repeated Mr. Burke. "The marine biologist? I've read many of your papers. I'm very interested in sharks."

Sarah's eyes closed. She waited for her grandfather's answer, sure that they had been caught.

"Really? Well, it is a small world!" responded Granddad, just as if they were meeting under perfectly normal circumstances. "This is my granddaughter, Sarah, and a friend of ours, Sonja. What brings you to the Keys? I haven't seen your boat here before."

Sarah's eyes flew wide open, and she watched in disbelief as Sonja and her grandfather carried on a lengthy conversation with Mr. Burke about sharks! She held the drink that Steve had brought her and held her tongue.

After they determined Sarah wouldn't need to go to the hospital, they toured the boat and then bid farewell to the two men.

As they walked back to the other side of the marina, they saw Bascum sitting on the railing of the Santos boat.

"Where've you been?" he bellowed when they were within hearing distance. "And what the heck happened up there? There were crab traps dropping all around me!"

"You won't believe this," Sonja began.

12

▼▼▼

Caught!

"Granddad, I've only got a week left!" moaned Sarah. "What if we don't catch them by the time I have to leave?"

"Sarah," Granddad cautioned his impatient granddaughter, "if we don't catch them, it means they aren't killing tens, maybe hundreds of sharks. Since your article came out, they may be lying low. Though since your last name is Marshall and not Santos, they might not realize you were the same girl that they met on their boat."

"That's true," Sarah admitted. "I wish they were meaner, Granddad."

"I know. I do, too. But they know they're breaking the law. I feel badly for other fishermen. Their role isn't as clear. Since humans have existed, we have depended on the sea. The Earth's oceans were so big and so full of life, we never imagined that there would be a time when they couldn't provide as much as we wanted to take. It's a difficult thing to change, Sarah."

"Well, we've got to change it," Sarah insisted. "I don't want to live in a world without sharks, Granddad."

"There's hope, Sarah," he said, looking at his granddaughter. "We're learning all the time. Look at Bascum, for Pete's sake. He used to be a poacher!"

Sarah laughed. She thought about the look on Bascum's face when she and Sonja told him what had happened. It was worth a few scrapes and a bump on the head just to see his reaction when they told him Sarah had been carried onto the very boat he was tagging.

Suddenly the radio crackled. "*Bssssstrrt*. Shark base, shark *bssstarr*. Come in."

Granddad jumped up and reached for the

black, oval microphone attached to the radio with a curly cord. He pressed the button on the side and spoke.

"This is shark base. Dr. Santos here. What's up?"

"We have a signal that the boat is out at the tool site. Our team reports a score."

"I'll call Connie. Meet you there," Granddad replied. "Tool" was code for hammerhead, and "Connie" was the code name for the Coast Guard. "This may be it, kiddo. I'll radio the Coast Guard. You tell Grandma what we're up to, and I'll get the boat ready."

Twenty minutes later they were flying, Granddad style, out to the same site where they had first seen the finning boat. Sarah was nervous. She felt the responsibility of the action they were taking. She knew it was the right thing to do, but it wasn't fun anymore.

By the time they arrived, the larger, faster Coast Guard boat was already there. The *Slippery Eel* had been boarded, and men were searching the cabins and the holds. Hector was arguing with the Coast Guard captain. Sarah and her grandfather pulled up close so they could hear the conversation.

"This is an exclusion area, and no one is permitted to shark fish until the reproductive season is over, you know that," said the captain. "And you're in a marine sanctuary—an underwater park!"

"We weren't shark fishing. Look in our hold. All we kept is red fish, and they're all legal size!" Hector was putting up a good argument. "I can't help it if a few sharks are hooked on our lines. We release them, I swear."

A large man in a uniform approached the captain.

"Sir, I believe we've got the goods. There's a large stash of frozen fins beneath the captain's water bed, sir. I can find no carcasses."

With that the two men were handcuffed. Sarah couldn't hear all that was going on, but she knew it wasn't good. Under the bed, she thought, the bed she had been lying on!

"What do they mean—no carcasses?" Sarah asked her grandfather.

"A shark's fins are about five percent of the total weight of the fish. You are allowed to keep the fins if you are fishing legally for whole sharks. In that case, the fins would be about five percent of your total catch. But they have *only* fins. Not good.

"Besides, this is a protected area, and this is the time of year little sharks like yours are born. We don't want people catching pregnant sharks. They have a hard enough time as it is," he added grimly.

As Sarah watched the scene on the other boat, Hector looked over and recognized Sarah and her grandfather. For a moment Sarah was frightened. Then Hector hung his head. He's ashamed, thought Sarah, and turned her head away. Then she thought, Well, he should be!

Other members of the Shark Guards began to arrive.

The Coast Guard captain took the two men onto the Coast Guard boat.

Sarah watched. Suddenly Bascum Washington appeared on the *Slippery Eel*.

"What's he doing there?" Sarah asked, surprised.

"He knows most of the Coast Guard guys," Granddad explained. "We'll get a lot more information out of him than from the radio."

Half an hour later Bascum's boat pulled up alongside theirs.

"Well, we caught 'em red-handed and then some," boomed a delighted Bascum. "They didn't have time to catch many sharks out here. They were just beginning to reel in their line. But there was a mess of frozen fins stored in chests under the bed. Real neat operation."

"Fins!" Sarah cried angrily, and then said in amazement, "Right under me!"

A sigh of relief escaped from her lips as the Coast Guard boat pulled away.

13
▼▼▼

Eye to Eye
with a Shark

A round them gulls called and dove. The
water sparkled. Sarah put on her polarized
sunglasses so she could see beneath the sheen of
the water. She thought about the sharks below.

"Granddad, why don't we all go for a shark
swim? I think we need some cheering up, and I
never got to see the sharks here, remember?"

Granddad smiled and called the others on
the radio. Within the hour many of the Shark
Guards were at the site. They all put on their
masks, snorkels and fins and slid overboard.
Chum appeared from several directions. The
group waited for a glimpse of something they

all understood was rare and beautiful.

A blacktip shark darted into the area. He seemed nervous to Sarah. He swam back and forth, grabbing a piece of chum. Then the Caribbean reef sharks appeared, moving quickly. One very large female snatched a piece of fish from the path of a smaller shark. The chum kept coming and the number of sharks increased.

The mood of the sharks was different today. Sarah watched her grandfather's reactions carefully. He didn't seem concerned. A female, at least ten feet long, shot out to the edge of the feeding area. Suddenly she was back. With a flick of her tail and a turn of her fin, she sped in and out of the chummed area. Soon she grew bolder, cutting in front of the other sharks to seize the hunks of fish and meat. Her flexible body swung in an S curve. Then the speed and movements of all the sharks began to pick up. Sarah feared there would be a feeding frenzy at any moment.

The big shark approached the line of swimmers. She swung her head from side to side and showed no fear of the humans. Sarah watched her grandfather and Bascum for any sign that things were getting out of hand. They still seemed unconcerned. Sarah's stomach muscles tightened.

The ten-foot shark came closer, and then still closer. She was heading directly for Sarah! Frozen, Sarah watched the shark approach. The shark was so close that Sarah could see the tiny pores around her head. She reached for her grandfather's hand. It was warm and strong.

Six inches from Sarah's mask the shark stopped and turned. Sarah was eye to eye with one of the fiercest predators on Earth. She willed herself to stay calm. She didn't wave her hands. She didn't flee back to the boat. Instead, she gripped her grandfather's hand and looked directly into the eye of the shark.

The shark twisted and dove. Sarah watched the flawless skin of the shark pass just inches beneath her. There was a hoot from the other snorkelers. They cheered for her. She had become one of them. Sarah relaxed and breathed deeply through her snorkel. Her grandfather gave her hand a squeeze and released it.

Then the big female reentered the arena.

Chum was still coming from several boats, and sharks were passing in all directions. Fins held down, the sharks cut their V-shaped tails from side to side. Heads bobbed and teeth flashed as they sawed through larger chunks of fish.

Next, the ten-foot female and a large male Caribbean reef shark sped toward the same hunk of chum. The female snatched it first. More chum fell nearby, and the two sped toward each other again. Neither gave way. Right in front of Sarah the two crashed together with a deafening sound. Sarah's fists were cramped from holding the rope so tightly. Again she watched the others to see what she should do. No one left the water. Sarah prepared herself for the worst. She held on. She waited . . . and waited. And . . .

Nothing happened. The conflict was over. The two sharks sped off into deeper water.

"Phew," mumbled Sarah, relieved that everything had ended so well. She turned to go back to the boat, but just then two great hammerheads entered the circle of snorkelers. The hammerheads circled slowly. Their eyes set at

each end of the "hammer" were uniquely posi-
tioned to see their world. Sarah wondered,
Why are they so different? Were they smarter
or better than the other sharks somehow? Sarah
watched as they fed on the few remaining
pieces of chum, scanned the line of swimmers
and swam off into the shadows.

The chum was gone. The remaining sharks'
movements became smoother and more relaxed.
Slowly sharks and humans left the spot where
for a few minutes the two top predators on
Earth had met without incident.

14
▼▼▼

Looking
Back

When Sarah and her grandfather got home, the phone was ringing.

"I'll get it," shouted Sarah as she threw down her backpack and armful of towels and gear. She grabbed the phone and said hello.

"Mom!" Sarah exclaimed, and signaled her grandfather to pick up the other phone.

"Hi there," said Joe, greeting his daughter when he got to the phone in his study. Sarah and her grandfather could see each other across the hall. "What did you say? You read Sarah's article?" He smiled over at Sarah. "Yes, it was very good. Very effective, too. As a matter of fact, we caught the finners today!" There was a long pause.

"Yes, it *was* the one Sarah wrote about. Now, now, calm down. She was never in any danger. She's just fine, aren't you, Sarah?"

"I really am fine, Mom. Guess what! I got to swim with live hammerheads today!" For a moment Sarah stopped to think how odd it was that in her family swimming with hammerheads would be considered a good thing.

Granddad's weathered face broke into a wide smile. "Yes, Sarah's done very well with the sharks."

"Mom, you never told me I would be swimming with sharks this summer! You didn't know? What? Come home early? No!" Sarah looked over at her grandfather. "We've still got so much to do."

"Things have turned out very well," Granddad said, looking back at Sarah. "In fact, I was going to ask Sarah if she wanted to come back next summer."

"Mom, may I?" Sarah begged. She thought about how much had happened since the beginning of the summer, when she couldn't wait to get home.

"Yes? Great! I love you, too." Tears crept into Sarah's eyes. "Yep, I'll see you soon. Love to Dad! 'Bye!"

Grandfather and granddaughter put down the phones and walked across the hall toward each other.

"Thanks, Granddad," said Sarah, hugging him. "For the best summer I've ever had."

"To tell you the truth, it worked out a lot better than I thought it would!" Granddad admitted. His hand shook slightly as he awkwardly patted Sarah's head. "After I retired, I didn't think I would ever swim with sharks again. So it was a surprise for both of us."

"Can I really come back next summer?" asked Sarah.

"Absolutely." Granddad had that serious, determined-scientist look that Sarah now understood. Sarah knew it meant he was already planning his next shark venture. She waited.

"Do you realize how many sharks are killed each year in fishing nets?" Granddad exclaimed. "Thousands! Those giant drift nets used for commercial fishing smother tons and tons of

sharks—as well as every other kind of fish. There's a lot of work to be done, and I could use your help!"

"I'm ready!" Sarah replied happily.

Sarah's grandfather smiled and shook his

head. "There goes my retirement," he groaned.

"You didn't like it anyway," Sarah reminded him.

"Hey, how about that female reef shark?" said Granddad, changing the subject. "Did you get a close enough look at her?"

"Yes. I know what it feels like to look into the eye of a shark now," said Sarah. "I always thought it would be like looking into the eye of a robot—something mechanical and cold—but it's different. Now I know that they're looking back."

▼▼▼

A Note from the Author

I have always been fascinated by sharks, partly because they seem so scary. I remember the moment I glimpsed my first shark. I was snorkeling in the Florida Keys. The shark appeared just beyond the reef, where the water became deeper. It appeared and disappeared so quickly, it left me with the feeling that it might have been just a flickering of light through the water. That instant, however, was enough to plant a tiny seed of curiosity. What were sharks really like? If they were as dangerous as their reputation suggested, why wasn't I gobbled up in that brief encounter?

Over the years scientific research has revealed that sharks are not the bloodthirsty, evil creatures we once thought them to be. As I worked on this book, I learned that sharks are highly evolved and more intelligent than I had thought. After watching the sharks at the National Aquarium in Baltimore, I tried to form a new vision of these incredible animals. However, every time I sat down at the computer to write, the theme from *Jaws* would play in my head, "Dum-dum, dum-dum." Soon the story would become scarier and scarier, until finally there would be a child about to fall into the water just as the shark rose to the surface and . . . I'd have to stop. That was not the story I wanted to write, but I couldn't help it. It was the story I believed in my heart, despite all my reading.

I decided that I needed either to go experience sharks in their environment or to write a different book. At the recommendation of Dr. Alan Henningsen at the aquarium in Baltimore, I made arrangements to attend Dr. Samuel H. Gruber's shark biology course at the Bimini Biological Field Station in the Bahamas. It was a course that included swimming with sharks.

Dr. Gruber couldn't have been a better advocate for sharks. After more than twenty years of research he knew sharks literally inside and out. Within two hours of landing on the tiny island of Bimini, we were in a boat headed to a site where we would see Caribbean reef sharks.

Poised on the side of the boat, waiting to enter the water where I *knew* there would be sharks, was my most difficult moment. I had to ignore every scary story I had ever heard about sharks and just jump. When the sharks arrived, I relaxed. They were silent, solemn, beautiful. I finally began to believe what I had learned from my research: that sharks are not terrors but exquisite animals that deserve our greatest respect.

Then there was the problem of what information to include in this book and what to leave out. I had to leave out so much! So I hope you will use some of the resources I've listed at the end of this book and discover even more about sharks.

I realize that not everyone wants to go swimming with sharks. And unless you go with someone who is very knowledgeable and experienced, you probably *shouldn't* swim with them! However, short of jumping into shark-filled waters, you can learn about them through stories, research, films and the great aquariums that are being built today.

With your help people can change the way they think about sharks. And if we can protect sharks, who knows what the benefits might be? An understanding of cancer? A healthy ocean? Or will we let sharks disappear from the Earth and never know all that they have to teach us? Only the future will tell.

Groups to Contact
for Information About Sharks
and How to Help Them

Please note that E-mail addresses are subject to the whims of cyberspace and may change or be somehow altered. There should be enough information in these addresses for you to find other sites if these do not work.

American Elasmobranch Society Web Page
http://www.elasmo.org/

Bimini Biological Field Station
9300 SW 99th Street
Miami, FL 33176–2050

Center for Marine Conservation
1725 De Sales Street NW, Suite 600
Washington, DC 20036
http://www.cmc-ocean.org/index.html

Fiona's Shark Mania
http://www.oceanstar.com/shark

A Few Places to See Sharks

American Zoo and Aquarium Association
http://www.aza.org
(Click on "AZA Members" to find the aquarium
nearest you.)

Aquarium of the Americas
1 Canal Street
New Orleans, LA 70130–1152
or P.O. Box 4327
New Orleans, LA 70178-4327
http://www.auduboninstitute.org/html/
aa_aquariumain.html.

John G. Shedd Aquarium
1200 South Lake Shore Drive
Chicago, IL 60605–9825
http://www.sheddnet.org/home.html

Monterey Bay Aquarium
886 Cannery Row
Monterey, CA 93940–1085
http://www.mbayaq.org/

National Aquarium in Baltimore
501 E. Pratt Street, Pier 3
Baltimore, MD 21202-3194
http://www.aqua.org

New England Aquarium
Central Wharf
Boston, MA 02110–3399
http://www.neaq.org/

SeaWorld Adventure Parks:
  SeaWorld California
  500 SeaWorld Drive
  San Diego, CA 92109–7995
  http://www.seaworld.com/seaworld/
    sw_california/swcframe.html

  SeaWorld Florida
  7007 SeaWorld Drive
  Orlando, FL 32821–8097
  http://www.seaworld.com/seaworld/sw_florida/
    swfframe.html

  SeaWorld Texas
  10500 SeaWorld Drive
  San Antonio, TX 78251–3002
  http://www.seaworld.com/seaworld/sw_texas/
    swtframe.html

7B